Shouldn't Play with Dead Things

Christopher Ridge

Published by Christopher Ridge, 2023.

SHOULDN'T PLAY WITH DEAD THINGS

First edition. May 29, 2023.

Copyright © 2023 Christopher Ridge.

ISBN: 979-8223112280

Written by Christopher Ridge.

SHOULDN'T PLAY WITH DEAD THINGS

That is what Timmy's mother told him that day she caught him with the dead cat.

"How many times do I have to tell you to stop playing with dead things? It's bad for your health."

Timmy swung the cat round and round by its tail then smacked it on the concrete driveway until every bone in its scull crushed. He liked listening to snap, crackle and pop. "But I killed it first."

"That's no reason to play with it. That's why you don't have any friends."

"I have all the friends I need."

His mother bit her lower lip and shook her head. "You scared poor Sally to death she's afraid to walk past the house."

"She's a sissy anyway. Never liked her."

"Well, Buck does everything in his power to avoid walking past our house and he lives next door. Saw him walk around the other end of the block. He won't even cross the street."

"He's a bully. Gets what he deserves."

She didn't tell him about all the letters she got from the school about how Timmy wasn't allowed to come to school anymore and now she has to homeschool him. The school caught him playing with a dead body in a casket hours before the funeral. Apparently, Timmy had got bored on the playground and went to he cemetery down the street from the school. He dug the grave, opened the casket and started playing with the arms and legs of the skeleton. Luckily one of the parents saw him, recognized him and sent for the principle.

Yeah, that one cost her several hours at a therapist appointment.

Then the science teacher, Mr. Radford decided to drop dead of a massive heart attack and Timmy was poking at his stomach with a stick trying to get him to fart.

The ambulance arrived, saw him doing this and that cost his mother more hours of therapy sessions.

"Your son is just downright scary," the principle said. "He scares all the kids."

His mother thought this was all just a little phase he was going through and that he would eventually grow out of it.

As he got older this wasn't happening.

Got worst.

Neighbors would start missing.

Search parties were in progress.

Nobody ever found any of the neighbors.

His mother did. She found them in her basement piled in what used to be an old potato barn that had its own entrance.

Timmy liked to play with the decomposing bodies like they were dolls.

He had them all arranged around the table. He'd changed their clothes out and mix match.

He'd put women clothes on men.

Men clothes on women.

He'd sew women arms on men and vice versa.

He'd even cut off women and man parts and sew them different bodies. Which always gave him the biggest kicks over that one.

His other flipped a lid when she went down there and saw what he had done.

She told him he couldn't keep on doing this. He had to stop.

"It's fun."

"I know it may seem fun, but its wrong. We're going to get locked up for a long long time if we get caught. If you get caught."

She found neighbors, dogs, cats, even a goldfish. It was like he'd created his own little town.

She had to put an end to this for sure.

Police were constantly knocking at the door. It was only a matter of time before a detective had enough tips that would encourage him to search even further.

Fortunately, the potato barn had its own secret entrance from the basement. A small square door in the wall was covered by a hollow block which Timmy had found by accident while he was chipping away at the block trying to see what was on the other side.

"It's going to be okay, Mother. Nobody will ever find me little playhouse."

"Then promise me you'll stop this now."

"I promise. I'll only play with the dead things I have."

This would've made his mother feel a ton better had he not been the type that had such a low attention span.

"I'm serious, Timmy. You have to stop this. I'm too old to go to prison."

"You're not going to prison."

By then Timmy had turned forty-five and still playing downstairs.

Every once in a while, somebody would be missing. Except now Timmy had gotten smarter and went to other towns. It also made things easier when he got his drivers license which allowed him to snag tourists where people came to visit all the shops during the fall.

Timmy had this craving. He just couldn't stay away from his dead toys.

He loved the rotten odor of farts and rotten eggs their decomposing bodies gave off.

He loved to listen to the creaking and cracking of their bones while he played with them as their skin slowly fell off.

It was really a lot of fun to watch the hair change color and fall out. Poke the eyes in further in the scull with a stick.

He even tried one once.

Didn't taste bad.

Felt slimy, and squished when he chewed it. It was like eating a gummy bear filled with blood.

As the kids that grew up in the neighborhood got older and had their own families, they would warn their kids to stay from the house.

A bad kid lives there. Though not now a kid.

And his mother.

She saw the whispers in the street and overheard several conversations at the grocery store.

She dared not take Timmy out in public. She couldn't.

She thought about leaving him.

Could lock him down in his playhouse where he would die with all his other playthings, but she couldn't stomach the idea of killing her son.

So, she left him down there where he was protected.

Maybe, he would just end up dying and it would put an end to all of it. He was gaining weight over the years. He couldn't move around as much as he used to. Though, by now, that was understandable because he was sixty and she was ninety. She was hardly in the shape to do anything.

Now, she had to rely on Timmy. But he managed to provide.

She'd lie in bed at night and she could hear Timmy down in his playhouse. Talking to his dolls, he called them.

He would slam them around on the floor from time to time.

Cursing at them pretending he was a wife abuser. One of his favorite games.

The creepiest was when he liked to pretend, he was a child molester.

Every night she would lie there and wonder what she had done to deserve a child that was so sick and twisted.

That night she heard the door to the basement open. Usually this meant Timmy was coming up to say good night before bed.

He opened her door.

What she expected was Timmy to enter with puckered lips and a cup of her evening tea.

Instead he was holding an axe.

Timmy stared at her for what seemed like several minutes.

Blood trickled from the corner of his mouth. "My family misses their mother."

NOT IN MY HOUSE YOU'RE NOT

Marge hated those things but she would be damned if she were going to allow them inside her house to beat her to death.

Not to mention, Tom, a big fat mean neighbor with a greasy, hairy belly that thinks he runs the neighborhood was bashing Fred's scull in with a hammer in the middle of the street.

WHACK...WHACK...WHACK...

His lips curled in a snarl as he banged so hard she could see the hammer sticking in his scull and Tom having to work to pry it out as if he were prying a nail out of a board.

Of all neighbors to get whacked he was not the one that deserved it. It just proved Marge's point. Nice guys do finish last.

No way are they getting in here.

The house she kept clean. The house her husband, Mike came home to after a long hard day at the office.

The house she raised her kids in.

The house they finally got paid off so Mike didn't have to work as much and could finally cut back on his hours at the truck company.

"I'm no spring chicken but I can duke it out with the best of ya," she yelled at them through the window.

The rednecks moaned and groaned. Their teeth yellow and nasty. She could only imagine what their breath smelled like especially, after eating all that flesh and other human body parts they shouldn't be eating.

Considering these were redneck crazies they'd be all up inside the liver and intestines just like her father liked to eat. He was the only one she knew who would actually eat those pickled pigs feet she'd seen in the jar on the shelves at Bo's gas station.

Crazies bumped into the window. There were a lot more of them today. They arrive in packs. Some days she wouldn't see any, others there would be four or five trying to get in.

"Not today." She poked at them with the broom hoping to shoo them away from the window.

The rednecks moaned and groaned.

Wait a second. She stared at the redneck's face. She saw a chunk of flesh hanging in the gap between his split front teeth. "Henry. Henry Thompson, is that you?"

Moans and groans followed by banging on the window.

"I thought I recognized you. I'm so sorry this happened to you. But there's no way you're getting in so you might as well just get."

Moans and groans as crazy redneck, Henry licked his lips and what remained of his yellow teeth he did have.

Next thing she knew six or seven more showed up, all of them banging at the large living room window.

She tried to get Mike to board the windows up but the crazies had got him that day he went to the store to get more supplies.

They came upon so fast.

Hardly any warning and the news didn't know much about what was going on at the time.

People had no idea why all of a sudden some people were walking around so slow and weird like as if they'd come down with a bad flu bug.

It was a bad bug all right, she thought.

Then people started eating whomever just happened to be in the parking lot at the time. Poor souls.

She knew this was going to pass eventually. But right now, there was no way they were getting inside her house.

No way was she going to allow them to.

Why, so they can dirty it all up and leave nasty marks everywhere.

"I dare yas! I dare ya! To try and get in here."

It was almost like they actually heard her because that made them bang on the window even more.

Those redneck crazies didn't have a clue who they were screwing with.

Marge was not going to lie down easy. She did not spend twelve years in the Marine Corps for nothing.

KILL ..KILL...KILL...

And I'm a gonna do some killin'

It started with the dark yellow cloud. You could see it forming in the distance. New reports were flooded from the next town over warning everybody that the cloud had something sinister inside it that was turning people into madmen with a vicious and uncontrollable appetite for human flesh.

The cloud was approximately ten miles wide and covered the entire town of Bargersville IN.

Mike called her on the phone from the grocery and told her what he'd saw.

Farmers bashing each other's brains out with garden hoes and rakes. Some tore down houses with their tractors. Others drove their pick-up trucks through houses like a bunch of Japanese Kamikaze pilots.

Some were drinking Pabst Blue Ribbon while driving their tractors over people.

She could hear the nervous tone in Mike's voice. He was scared and she could hear the sound of chainsaws and motors in the background.

"Mike, get out of there and get home..." Was the last thing she said before she heard the rev of the saw and Mike screaming.

According to her friend, Mable, the crazy cloud lasted for five hours. If you can manage to survive five hours then the cloud passes on to the next town. In their case hopefully it fades away.

The house turned a dark shade of yellow inside. And outside the cloud was centered over the town.

A pack of crazies were walking down the street. Some of them dressed in jean coveralls and looked as if they'd just come in from the fields. There were fifteen or twenty of them. Each of them carried their own tool of choice.

Garden hoes. Hammer. Sledge hammer. Chainsaws. She saw one with golf clubs and knew right away that was Mike's golfing buddy, Stewart. Blood dripped off the clubs as if he'd just got finished whacking somebody.

Stewart's eyes were red and he was walking with a purpose.

They all walked with a purpose.

They were walking straight toward her house.

"No way. Tell me you are not coming here."

She didn't know why they chose her house over all the other ones on the street other maybe it might've had something to do with Mike being friends with everybody. Mike was one of those neighbors everybody loved.

Poor Mike. If only he would've listened to her and came home when she told him.

Men these days.

He had to get some more wood, he said because he needed to reinforce the front door and needed more nails. She tried to tell him that it was enough and they would have to make due with what they had and couldn't afford him being caught out in the crazy wave.

At the Wal-Mart non the less. How many times had she told him to stay away from that place?

There had already been six shootings and there was practically a fight every day.

If I were the Mayor, I'd burn the stupid thing to the ground she'd said. The Wal-Mart was bad enough but then some idiot had to go and bring in a liquor store and then a couple months later a pawn shop.

There went the neighborhood. It was all down hill from there.

A large group of them gathered around Gayle's house. Climbing in through the windows. Two of them were on the roof going down the chimney.

The two climbing through the window had pick axes.

Ohhhh, poor Gayle. This is just going to be awful. Feel so sorry for her.

Gayle had lost her legs due to diabetes and was stuck in a wheelchair. She was also severely overweight and on oxygen.

No way was she going to stand a chance.

I am not going to put up with these things, she said. If they're going to come and get me they're a gonna get a fight.

I'll be damned if they're going to come in here tearing my house up. They don't know who they're screwin' with.

She grabbed her old Marine Corp helmet and strapped it on. She hadn't worn this thing in years. Sure felt good to have it on. Looking at herself in the mirror she gave one of those Marine Corps I'm a killer snarls.

The gun storage cabinet was in the corner of their bedroom. There were two AR's and a Glock and a lot of ammo.

She wasn't sure how long it was going to last but hopefully once they see she isn't to be reckoned with they'll back off.

Naaa. Unfortunately, it didn't look like it was going to be that easy.

Forty to fifty of them flooded the streets.

Then here came farmer Jones in his John Deere tractor plowing down the street. She watched as he ran off the road and made a turn for Julie's house and plowed right through the front door. Ten crazies ran in through the large opening.

Ohhh, heck no. No way. I dare yas to try that. I just dare yas.

She didn't know what she would do if they tried that but she would figure something out.

The sky was lightening up and the inside of the house was getting brighter. But if all the calculations were right she still had two hours left of this nonsense.

Two hours of watching these redneck crazies busting down doors and windows and her hoping for the best.

Outside there was a lot of hootin' and hollerin' and the sound of glass breaking. Women screaming.

Five of them were smashing the Hyundai Sante-Fe across the street.

"You suckers are in for it now. You messin round here you see."

She watched on as they continued to bash and smash everything that was in their way.

"I am not going to let you in."

She knew it was coming. There were just too many of them.

Then came the banging on the door.

Grunting and groaning sounds..

BANG BANG BANG

"Go away. You hear me. You don't want non of this."

More banging. Grunting and groaning.

An arm smashed through the center of the door. It was hairy. Sweaty. Her heart beat quickened.

The fingers wiggled their way toward the door latch hoping to find it.

She smashed the hand with the butt of the rifle.

"I'm warning you to get back."

The door busted off the hinges and there stood at the doorway the ugliest redneck she'd ever saw. He was fat, no shirt and had a beer belly the size of Mt. St Hellen.

He smiled a toothless smile, licking his lips as if she were a piece of chicken.

She aimed toward his gut and fired, blowing a hole in the center of his belly as he landed on the floor with a thud.

Five to six more followed.

All of them smirking as if they'd just won the grand prize.

"Get away from here. All of ya's. You hear me."

They walked toward her not paying her any attention to the gun she held and pointed at them.

She fired and hit one in the head, and he went down.

Fired again and hit another.

"Look at that. You're standing on my clean carpet with those nasty feet. Not only were they dirty but looked like toe fungus had been growing on them for decades. Get those things off my carpet."

She fired and he went down. This one stumbled and staggered more onto the white carpet. It took her another two shots before he finally went down and landed on her clean carpet and started bleeding to death.

"Good God gracious. What a mess. I told you morons you weren't messing up my house."

She backed up the stairs. If she could managed to get upstairs, she could make it to the attic and lock herself in there.

The rednecks's greasy hands left prints all over her wall and knocking down her pictures.

One of them fell over the handrail from leaning on it with all his weight as he walked up the stairs and ripped if off the wall and tumbled down to the bottom of the stairs.

She fired three. Four more times.

Hitting each one of them in the head splattering their brains all over her walls.

"Lord mercy. This is making such a mess."

She was pissed because her and Mike just painted those walls just a couple weeks ago. A light brown paint with white trim. She just thought it looked nice and went with the furniture.

Which she'd just replaced that just a few weeks before painting. Her and Mike had bought this nice brown couch and an extra loveseat with all the nice hidden compartments where she could store her comfort blankets. Mike had a section that was all for his remotes and a place for his cold beer.

Now it was all ruined because two of the rednecks were walking all over it, Jack Daniels bottles in hand dripping it all over the couch leaving their dirty filthy prints everywhere and, in some areas, tearing it.

"Uggggg," She yelled like a Marine at the battle of Iwo Jima. "All over my new couch. You idiots know how hard it is to get those stains out?"

She had a few words and blasted them.

The rednecks threw Pabst Blue Ribbon cans and Coors lite bottles at her. One of the bottles knocked her in the head and the redneck chuckled all toothless and fat.

Marge shook it off. "You couldn't hit with anything heavier than that mountain piss?"

She aimed and blasted'm.

"Serves you only right."

She emptied the magazine and reloaded it.

The more she shot the more the rednecks came to take their place. It was like the never-ending redneck apocalypse.

She could tell the sun was shining inside the house that the evil yellow cloud was starting to lift.

If only I can make it, she thought.

The clock on the wall showed that she had approximately fifteen minutes left. She wondered how this was going to end. Would the rednecks just calm down all of sudden and walkway?

But that meant she had at least fifteen more minutes of shooting to do and she had to admit she was having a blast. What a great stress relief. She hadn't done any descent killing since desert storm.

Wow was this a blast.

She sure did have a job on her hands cleaning all this mess up. Sure, was going to take some time.

She settled in upstairs and continued to blast away the rednecks one by one as they came through the door.

Sometimes five at a time.

Chewing their tobacco and spitting all over her carpet and floors.

Disgusting.

Mike chewed for a while. Dipped that Copenhagen snuff. She remembered how she used to always get after him for leaving his cans of spit everywhere.

And his breath. Oh, God. His breath stunk at times and then he'd try to kiss her and all she wanted to do was punch him in the face.

"You rednecks have no decency for human beings I tell yas. No respect."

A big fat one grinned a toothless grin, spat on the step, grabbed hold of her foot and pulled her down the stairs.

She kicked and fought with the other foot. She thought he was going to yank her down the steps but instead he put her foot to his mouth and bit her toes. What remained of his teeth chomping down on her big toe.

It took her a moment to realize she was still holding the gun. She pulled the trigger and blasted him in the head splattering his redneck brains all over her what was once nice walls.

Her big toe was now bitten down to a stub causing her extreme pain as she scooted up the stairs.

Rednecks charged through the door licking their lips as if they were at Big John's Barbeque and grill.

"Come on in. Mama has a surprise for ya all."

Rednecks grinning with their tobacco filled mouths, inhaling, and exhaling through their noses sounding like a bunch of bulls.

By now there are at least thirty of them in her house. She could hear dishes breaking in the kitchen. The sound of glass breaking, and pots and pans being knocked around.

It was too late.

She realized now that there was no possible way of protecting her nice house any longer.

But she wasn't going to let it stop her from taking out as many as she could.

One by one she picked them off.

And one by one their brains splattered.

Guts poured.

But more kept coming.

One of them was Thelma, her sewing partner. "Oh, Thelma. Not you too."

Their arms outstretched holding their beer cans.

She aimed.

"Go to hell! Everyone of of yas can go to hell!"

Click.

Click.

Clickety Click

LOVING HER

Harold Butler stood on the corner of the alley by Taps Tavern when he saw his finance, Janet getting banged by some other dude.

At first, he staggered past them. He felt fine while he was sitting at the bar but the second, he got up and went outside and everything started moving. They had been drinking all evening and committed the biggest sin ever of not eating anything, so the booze went straight to his head.

The cool misty rain and the fog provided a nice relief, but it caused him to miss the corner where his car was, and he went down the wrong side street and that's when he saw them.

Mouth wide.

Speechless.

They were supposed to get married in three weeks.

Janet was the love of his life. Known her since high school.

He saw her talking to him before but never thought anything of it. After the fifth time he became curious. Especially when she told him she had to go the restroom and would meet him back at the car in a couple minutes.

For some reason he got this upset feeling in his stomach. That feeling something was wrong. Not right.

He didn't want to think that. He wanted to trust her. What good is a marriage if you can't trust your partner? They were going to spend the rest of their lives together.

And he was right.

Here it was two in the morning, closing time, and he's standing out in the rain watching.

Her so-called secret lover's pants down to his ankles. Janet, propped up against the wall.

He could hear her moaning.

Groaning.

He was grunting as he looked like a jack rabbit pounding away with uncontrollable force.

Should I say something?

Do something.

He wiped the seat from around his forehead. As of right now, he felt like puking.

Maybe I should clear my throat or cough or something. Let them know that I now know.

No.

A rusty tire rod just happened to be lying at the side of the building.

How convenient.

It would be so easy right now to walk up behind him and whack him in the head. My luck, as big as he is, would take me a couple good whacks to get him down.

Maybe if I were bigger. Stronger.

He'd never been the jock type. Never played any sport. He was not even well known in school. Always kept low key.

He wished he was stronger. Braver even.

Is this what happens when you keep low key? Somebody else comes along and steal your girlfriend?

His chest felt like somebody was grabbing his heart from the inside and squeezing the blood out of it as if it were a rag.

He gasped as he took a minute to catch his breath. Then he walked back to the car.

He could see how this was all going to go down.

Like this...

She would come back to the car as if nothing happened. Give him a kiss and tell him how much she loved him. She'll want to go get an early breakfast where they will discuss their plans for getting married.

She was the one with all the plans, not him. Having grown up with two sisters he knew how important a nice wedding was, so he just let her do her thing and was pretty much open to anything.

Because he wanted her to be happy.

He wanted to make sure she had nice things.

Watching this made him feel like puking. Upset tummy coupled with too many Jim Beam and cokes than he could really handle.

He went back to the car.

Thought about driving away and leaving her there.

Why not?

Obviously, she didn't really care for him.

How long have we been dating?

Well, he'd known her since high school. They both went their separate ways after graduation. He was at college for two years, of which he realized college wasn't for him. She stayed home and worked at some store with her mother. They got together not long after he came back home, which was three years ago. Just last year, he popped the marriage question and they'd been planning it ever since.

Until this...

His thinking was interrupted when the door opened.

"High, sweetie," she says. "Sorry it took so long." She gave him a quick peck on the cheek.

Her breath smelled. Like whiskey, beer and another man's breath. For some reason he could tell. He could smell some sort of cologne. Aftershave perhaps.

Hmmm. He didn't think he was the kind of guy who'd wear aftershave. Aqua Velva. For some reason the thought made him chuckle.

"Everything ok?" She fastened her seat belt and adjusted her bra. "You look different."

Hmmm. Different like how?

He wanted to say. Of course, I'm different, bitch. I saw you screwing some other dude behind the bar.

But he didn't.

Instead, he took the wimpy way out and said. "Fine. Too much to drink I suppose."

He chuckles. There was a time when he thought her little childish chuckles were cute.

Now, they were irritating.

He couldn't stand the sight of her. Her lipstick was smeared on her face. He could see where she tried to touch it up, but it was still smeared. Her skirt was wrinkled. She was missing an earring.

He sniffed.

Plus, he could smell the other man on her.

Visions of him butt naked pounding on her were forever planted in his mind.

Somebody has to pay for this.

He didn't ask for those kinds of memories. Memories that were never going to leave.

There was no way he was going to be able to marry her now. No way. His marriage was ruined.

His life was ruined.

He'd planned on having children with her. Raising kids in a nice big house on Hemlock Way.

He decided to ask. More like play along. "What took so long?"

"I was just talking to a friend I ran into."

And there it was.

A lie.

All a lie. A nasty lie that came off the tip of her tongue as if it were nothing.

A lie done to perfection.

No expression. No hesitation.

A like done so well he would have believed it if he hadn't saw what he saw.

He gripped the wheel so tightly his knuckles turned white.

She put her hand on his cheek. "You okay, sweetie. We can get a room at that Days Inn if you don't feel like driving."

"I'm fine."

He was more than sober now. He lost his high after seeing what he saw.

Her touch was disgusting.

Gross.

Did you touch his penis with that hand?

He couldn't stand to even look at her now but as odd as it felt at the time, he for some reason still loved her.

He had no idea why.

Is this what true love feels like? If it is I don't think I can handle it.

He pulled up to her house and put the car in park. He let out a deep sigh. If he was going to have to be careful how he handled this situation.

This was not easy, but it was going to have to be something he had to do. He had to make things right.

Have to take care of that dude. Got to fix this and then she would come back to me.

After all this is what happens. It all starts with cheating and then the next thing you know she's going to tell him the dreaded words.

We need to talk.

Then comes. We should take a break from each other.

He was going to take a break all right but not until he fixed this mess. He learned enough from his sisters that sometimes women screw things up and it needs to be fixed. His sisters were good women, but they were taken advantage of.

He was not going to allow this to happen.

Nobody was going to take advantage of his Janet. That man she was having sex with, no matter how much it hurt him, he wasn't going to love her like he does.

He wasn't going to give her things like he is.

He doesn't respect her like he does.

How does he know this? Because no man who respects a woman will not bang her in the back alley of a bar, zip his pants up and say thanks a bunch that was fun. We should get married.

The dude was clearly a wife beater. It wouldn't surprise him if he had a family. He didn't have to know him to know this. It just goes without saying because of the lack of respect she gave her.

Why couldn't Janet see this?

Because she didn't want to see this. He probably fed her a bunch of nonsense crap about how pretty and how beautiful on the inside she was.

She kissed his cheek and opened the door. "Have a good night, sweetie." She looked at him as if something was wrong. "You sure everything is all right?"

"Fine. Just have a lot on my mind."

"Don't think so much. You know thinking is dangerous."

When he got home, he got undressed and lay on the bed staring at the ceiling. At three in the morning, he should've been passed out the second he collapsed on the bed. Instead, he lay staring at the ceiling.

Something didn't seem right about this. She showed no signs of trying to hide what he'd seen.

Is this the first time she'd done this or had she been doing this all along and he just happened to find out?

So many questions he asked himself.

I have to fix this. Just don't know how.

The next day he stayed home to nurse his hangover and slept the rest of it off. When he woke, he was hoping that he was only dreaming and that it hadn't happened.

It did.

Some of the evening was a bit fuzzy. He wished he could've saw the dude's face more clearly though. Give him a good idea who it was. He was certain though he'd be able to recognize him if he saw him even though it was his bare butt.

Janet called him later to check up on him.

Her voice is still sweet.

Her lying voice.

He wanted to talk to her about this. At least confront her about it. He figured she would just lie to him. Say it never happened and that he was only imagining her getting banged behind the alley like a whore.

There was a way to fix it.

Forgiveness is key though. First, I have to forgive before I can fix it. He scrolled up to her picture on his phone. Enlarged it. "It's okay, Janet. I forgive you. I'm going to fix this so you will no longer be tempted by that evil creature. He doesn't love you like I do."

How. How am I going to do this?

Simple.

Get rid of him. Yes. Do that and that will eliminate the problem.

I should tell her what I'm going to do. Yes. That would be awesome. That way she will see how much I love her and that I will do anything to keep us together.

Yes. I'm certain she will love me even more.

Even more than him.

I should tell her now about my wonderful idea. He grabbed his phone and pressed her little image he had saved on his home screen.

Wait.

Not good.

Her phone rang but he hung up.

I should make it a surprise. A surprise to show her that I will do anything and that nobody is going to stand in our way.

I'll kill him and show her what I did. We will be bonded forever and ever.

It's going to be awesome.

She called back. "Hi, sweetie. Just saw you called."

No. Don't you tell her yet. "Just calling to say I love you."

"Ohhh, you're so sweet. I love you too."

"I also have a surprise for you."

"You do?"

"Not yet. But soon."

"What is it?"

"If I told you I'd have to kill ya."

She chuckled. This time it sounded much cuter than the time back in the car.

She was going to be so surprised when she sees what I've done for her. She is really going to know how much I love her.

It just so happened he was walking home from his job as a security officer at the dog food warehouse when he saw the dude that was banging his lover.

He was big. He hated to admit this but even his butt looked the same only this time with jeans on. He had on the same type of black jacket and his hair looked the same, at least from the back.

He was sure this was the dude.

He stayed back around the corner and let him get far enough ahead before he turned. Careful not to draw suspicion to himself.

Following him made it a lot easier to hide in the crowd of people walking on their way home and to the subways.

It was around six in the evening, so it was busy.

He wanted to know more about this guy. Where he came from. Did he work with Janet?

But it didn't matter. Soon this whole little escapade he had going on is going to be over.

Same tennis shoes, also.

He was certain this was his guy. One has to be very careful about such things when you're planning on torturing and killing someone. Such a mistake could have some horrifying consequences.

Janet was worth it though.

They were born to be together. They were meant for each other.

Harold followed him around the corner and watched him walk into Lucky's Pub.

Ohhhhh, yes. This was most definitely the guy.

Harold went inside. The guy didn't know who he was so he there wasn't any real threat.

Harold sat at the other end of the bar and drank a cola. No alcohol for him tonight. He needed to be on his best behavior and needed to keep himself intact.

But wow was he a big dude. At least six foot maybe an inch or two over. Arms like a football player.

Is this the kind of guy she really wants? Is this it? If so, I can fix that. I can start going to the gym and working out. I'll hire a body builder that can get me beefed up, oiled up nice and pretty. Sure, it will take a bit of work, but I can do it.

I'll do it for her.

For my Janet.

He watched the guy reach for his phone.

Ooops. Just thought of something. What if he's calling Janet and she meets him here?

That would be bad.

If she shows up, I can just say I stopped by on my way home. Nothing unusual about that. Or I can just sneak out the back door. Yes... That would probably be best.

Harold watches as another woman approaches the beefy dude. She has a smile on her face as if she's glad to see him.

She kisses him and he puts his arm around her, waits and pulls her closer to him.

Looky at that. He's already talking to another woman. Ohhh, you dirty dog. I would never consider doing that to my Janet. You don't deserve her even if she does choose you over me. Which she won't. I'm going to make sure of that. You just proved my point on what a dirt bag you are.

Harold waited in his car for what seemed like two hours. So badly he wanted a few drinks, but he wanted to do this, he had to be in good shape. This was not going to a walk in the park. He was tired. Exhausted.

Sure, he wanted to just go home and curl up under the covers, but the payoff was going to be well worth it.

It was two in the morning. Closing time. Harold was expecting him to walk out at any time.

He just hoped he didn't walk out amidst the crowd.

Need a plan B if that happens. Oh well. I'll cross that bridge when I get to it.

He watched as several young guys that didn't look to be much older than twenty-one get in their cars.

Shouldn't drink and drive, Harold thought, shaking his head, disgusted at what he was seeing.

At the far left a couple were in a Dodge Charger, the windows were fogging up and he could just barely make out a head floating up and down in arithmetic motion.

Finally, here he came. Harold watched him staggering a bit, swaying as he looked to be having a hard time opening his door. It looked like he kept pressing the lock button on his remote with the way it kept beeping.

This was the perfect opportunity.

Nobody around either, except for the couple getting it on in the Charger.

Harold drove up to him and parked by the side of his car. "Car trouble?"

"Naa. I'm good, dude. Thanks."

Harold eyed him up and down. He was a big dude. Even bigger up close. At least six foot and three hundred pounds.

Still shouldn't be a problem though. As drunk as he is.

Harold grasped the pipe as he held it close to his side. "Let me give you a hand with that."

"Look. Dude. I said I got this...."

"You got this all right. Good thing you're out cheating on your girl, my girl." He hated this guy even more now.

"What are you taking about?" His speech was slurred.

"Driving drunk. What if my, I mean your girl, who won't be for long I add was with you and you get in an accident and kill her? What then?"

All the chatter caused him to drop his keys. "Dude. I don't know what you're talking about. Do I know you?

"Kinda. Sorta."

"Get out of here fer I kicks your ass."

Harold whacked him in the head with the pipe when he bent down to pick up his keys.

Amazingly, the guy still didn't go down. Just said, "Owwwe."

Harold was like, Owwww. Is that all you got to say? But whacking a guy whose head is as big as an anvil is no easy task.

Harold whacked him again and again.

Three. Four times.

Each time harder. Telling himself the harder you hit the harder they fall.

The three or four whacks only brought the guy down to his knees. It was obvious to Harold that this guy had been in several altercations before. He was taking it so well.

Blood on the pipe.

Harder and harder Harold swung. Giving it everything he got. He felt like he was David fighting Goliath only in a much more brutal way.

Six. Seven times.

Harold heard his scull crack. He kept on going. Blood all over the back of the dude's head and dripping down along the side of his face puddling up on the ground beneath his hands.

One more whack did the trick and took him out. At least he hoped it was enough to take him out. Harold thought he saw the guy's chest still moving. Most likely that was just his lungs expelling the last big of air. No way could a guy survive such a beating.

Harold glanced around. The Dodge Charger was gone. He didn't even hear it leave. This was good because it was going to take some time to shove his big ass in his small Hyundai Accent.

He had to get this guy out of here. He had plans for him. Special surprise for Janet. Looking around he realized there was no way he was going to get this beast in his car.

Then he remembered he had an electric carving knife in the trunk. It was a Christmas present for his mother.

He opened the trunk, found the box and opened it.

He pressed the button.

Good. Surprised that it had some charge. Usually, this stuff has a little. Hopefully it was enough to get the job done.

He remembered seeing a couple plastic contractor bags.

Even better.

The electric knife came alive with a soft hum when he turned it on.

As he prepared the knife, he heard a moan. Groan.

No way. Dude moved.

You got to be kidding me. Now by all rights, he should be amazed by this guy's face right about now. But he didn't want to mess up his face. He had to at least keep him to a point so he could show Janet what he'd done.

He shrugged.

Commenced carving.

Started with the arms. Then legs. At first it was hard getting through the bone and the blade kept jamming and bending.

ZZZZZZ....... Zzzzzzzzzz.

He took a while, but he got through. The dude's leg was almost as big as his waist.

Now comes the fun part. Cutting off his head. Funny though, how the dude's mouth kept moving like a fish. You'd think he'd done bleed out by now.

He'd read somewhere that the brain stays alive a little longer even after the body dies.

Harold wondered what it must feel like to him right now.

He hoped that the dude was feeling excruciating pain beyond belief. This made him feel good I side as if he were doing something important.

Just wait till Janet gets a look at you now.

He sliced the head off. Watching the blade as it cut straight across is Addams apple and sinking fast. The knife jiggling and jarring in his hand as the blade jammed as it hit was, he thought would be the spinal cord.

He twisted the blade side to side careful not to break it.

The motor of the blade slowly to a soft hum and revved back to life.

The rest was just a matter of slicing through the rest of the meat like cutting it into a chicken.

He placed the head in a bag and threw it in his trunk.

He was about to place the other parts in a bag when he heard the hum of an engine in the distance and saw a small beam of light down the road.

He left everything as is and got in his car and took off.

Now, that could've been a real close call.

It was worth it.

The look on Janet's face was going to be priceless.

He kept the severed head on ice until the next evening.

He invited Janet over for dinner. Made her favorite, chicken parmesan and spaghetti. The head was the center piece covered in a stainless-steel serving tray.

The excitement of waiting all day was unbearable.

The time had come. Janet was here.

She looked lovely in her short red dress and that sweet perfume she liked but he could never remember the name of.

"Sorry I was late," she said. "The cops are all over the place. Have the traffic blocked off. Something about finding body parts hacked up."

"That's nuts."

"All kinds of sickos running around out here. Probably has to do with drugs I bet. It's always drugs."

Wait till she sees it was me all along. She's going to be solo shocked. "Hope you're hungry."

"Smells wonderful. Is this the surprise?"

"Part of it. You'll see ."

"You're always full of surprises. That's why I love you."

She'll love me even more when she sees what I've done for her.

He pulled the chair out for her like a perfect gentleman and slid her back in. He unfolded a napkin and placed it across her lap.

"Wow. What the occasion?"

"Just loving you. I have something special to show I think you will like."

She smiled. He lived the way she smiled. She was going to be so happy. "Can't wait to see what you came up with."

He lifted the lid on the tray revealing the severed head. TaDa."

Janet covered her mouth as she screamed.

"That was not the reaction I was expecting. I thought you would be happy."

"You did this?"

"Isn't he awesome."

"This is sick. You're sick."

"I thought you would be happy. I did this for you. For us "

"For us?"

"That's right. I saw him banging you two days ago in the alley behind the bar. At first, I was mad at you but then I thought that if I get him out of your life then, he'll be out of ours."

"So, you saw that, ha?" She lowered her head in shame "I was meaning to talk ...."

He put his hand up to stop her. But it's okay. I forgive you. It's not all your fault."

She laughed as if this whole thing was silly. Wait. You think this...?"

"Is the guy. This is funny to you?"

"As sick as it may seem. Yes."

"This is so great. I knew you would be happy. I was hoping you would like it "

"The only problem is, that isn't the guy. "

What?"

"Never saw him before in my life. You screwed up big time this time, Harold.

Now, he was confused. This was not good. Obviously, he was going to have to come up with a better plan.

Oh well. I'll do whatever it takes. One thing is for sure. Loving her sure could be a chore at times.

NEIGHBORHOOD WIFE SWAP

You know the type of neighborhood. Sure, you do. They're tucked away in the small corners of the suburbs. Everybody knows everybody and is all up in everybody's business. Sometimes a bit too much really. These types of neighborhoods are made up of hard-working folks. Each of them have their own set of struggles behind closed doors. Though the neighbors are often aware of each other's personal battles, still, they try their best to keep their meddling down to a minimum.

"Oh, this is going to be wonderful living here," Janet said. "Just how I pictured it would be."

A young man was walking his dog, smiled and waved in front of their new two-story house. Well, not really new. To them it was. The house was built in the early nineteen hundreds and was in the historic district. The mailman was whistling to some tune he seemed to be making up along the way. Then along came the ice-cream truck being chased down by four boys.

An old man was watching them from a top floor window. He smiled and waved. Janet could tell that hist teeth probably hadn't seen a dentist in quite some time.

This was the neighborhood Janet always dreamed of living in.

She grew up in a trailer in in Tempe Arizona, so moving to a small neighborhood in Indianapolis in a house like that was like, considered good living. She felt like they were rich.

Except for their marriage. This was the part that was rocky. Allen had a good job, worked hard as a Architect but his long hours away from home had put a toll on her. They hardly ever had any alone time. It was a quick peck on the cheek, and he was out the door and she didn't see him until late that night.

After years of living and feeling like a single woman who wasn't allowed to go out, she approached Allen one day about going to counseling.

He wasn't too keen on it at first because he thought everything was fine. Until after she explained how she couldn't continue to live like this, or she was going to file for a divorce and move on with her life.

Fortunately, Allen agreed on the whole counseling thing. He never realized his marriage was such a mess and he felt bad about it. He thought that he was doing a good thing by working hard and making sure she had plenty of shopping money. Actually, she never wanted for nothing. He gave her everything she needed or wanted except for the companionship part. The part he was failing in and didn't realize.

After several counseling sessions one day Allen came to Janet with a wallop of an idea.

They were going to move.

He was given a job opportunity at a much smaller firm. The hours would be shorter, the demands lighter. This would give them more time for each other.

Janet thought this was great that her husband was willing to work at keeping their marriage alive. A lot of her friends ended up in a divorce which if you have kids can be hard on them.

The house he found for them was in Indianapolis. When he saw the picture of the house on line he knew immediately it was going to be the house for Janet. She'd always dreamed of having a large two-story house of this nature so this was perfect.

She was going to love it.

They were going to love it.

He made an extra trip there to take a look at it, ended up sighing the papers for it while he was there, he was that sure of it.

A month after that they had been packed up and were in their new town and life could not get any sweeter.

They hadn't even had a chance to unpack anything when they received their first official visit, Janet Riley who lived next door just stopping by for a visit to introduce herself and welcome them to the neighborhood. And to invite Janet over for coffee one day.

Later Ralph Marshall stopped by. He and his wife just lived two houses down.

Then of course, no neighborhood gets by without having at least one Mayor. You know the nosy body who keeps the scoop on everybody. Her name was Anna and there wasn't a thing that didn't get by her. She warned them about Mike and Donna's kids who liked to walk the sidewalk at night peeking in cars and every once in a while. She told them they live in the raggedy house on the corner.

"Don't let your guard down around them kids," she said as she waved her finger. "Those kids are nothing but trouble."

Allen smiled. He pretended he was listening, desperately wanted her to leave but didn't want to be rude. He hoped they didn't get a lot of visits from her. Somehow, he didn't think that was going to be the case.

While they busied themselves moving the boxes around from room to room, as much as they felt like doing anyway, the doorbell rang.

It was Monica who lived across the street. She was holding a bag.

Allen called Janet over. "Another neighbor comes bearing gifts."

Monica smiled. She was tall, with long tanned legs that looked UMPTEEN delicious. Perfect hourglass shaped body sporting 'oh my God breasts.' The type that causes impure thoughts to race through your mind. "I saw you guys moving in earlier and wanted to take a minute and welcome you to the neighborhood." She handed Janet the bag. "I brought a little something for you. Hope you like it."

Janet smiled as she took the bag. "Thank you. But that really wasn't necessary."

"Oh, that's okay. It's not much. Just a little housewarming gift."

Janet wasn't sure about this woman. The way her blouse was low cut revealing far too much for her taste and the way she spoke all giddy. "Thank you very much. Would you care to stay a moment and have a drink?" She was trying to be polite but hoped she didn't accept.

Monica's eyebrows rose. "Oh, I can't. Take a rain check though. Club meeting is tonight."

"Oh, okay. Some other time then."

"Of course." Monica turned to walk down the steps when she stopped and turned around. "Oh, maybe you two would like to come to a meeting sometime. We have a lot of fun."

"Yeah, maybe we'll do that," Janet said.

"Great. We live right over there." She pointed to the house diagonal from theirs.

"What kind of club is it?" Allen asked.

Monica tilted her head back and forth in a bubbly ditsy fashion. "Oh, it's a small group of us where we play games, have a few drinks, and share about our marriages and we each come up with ideas of how we can add that little extra spark to our lives. You know? We tend to be so busy busy all the time. It's made a difference in mine and Hank's marriage. We were on the verge of divorce and all that... Oh I'm sorry. I'm boring you to tears aren't I. Silly me. Silly silly me. Anyways I won't keep you two. Don't want to bore you with all our troubles. You two look like you've got it all together. I think you're just going to love it here."

She turned and walked away. The sound of her red high heel shoes clicking on the sidewalk.

Janet couldn't refrain from watching Monica walk down the sidewalk. Her round butt twitching back and forth. Her body was sizzling hot and she knew it.

"Tell you one thing," Allen said. "She sure can talk."

"Ain't that the truth."

Allen clapped his hands. "So. What's in the bag?"

Janet gasped when she looked in the bag. She knew there was something different about that woman.

"What is it?" Allen asked.

"I don't think you want to know."

"The way you said that makes me want to know even more."

Inside there were a couple small bottles of sex lotions used to create that extra spark during performance. A pair of edible chocolate panties and a small can of whip cream.

Allen looked impressed. "Wow. I bet I know what she's in to."

"And she flaunts every bit of it too." It made her wonder what her husband was like. She was sure they were going to meet him soon.

That night they turned in early. After spending the day getting the boxes inside and that long visit from Monica, they were exhausted.

But of course, a young couple such as they can't let their first night go by without christening the house with a night of great sweaty sex. Come on. First night in a new house you have to have sex.

To throw a little more shock into their relationship Allen suggested they have kids in this big house.

He told her he could see little Allen juniors and tiny Janet in cute pink dresses running through the hall, sliding down the hand rails.

Sledding down the stairs on a blanket.

Janet was ecstatic. The more he talked like that the hornier she became.

She ripped his clothes off and they had hot steamy sex in the middle of the living room floor. Needless to say, they didn't get much sleep that night either.

It didn't take long to meet Monica's husband. He was out raking leaves in his yard when he saw Janet out in the yard thinking about the landscaping flower arrangement, she was planning on working on next summer. When she saw him, he was every bit of what she imagined.

He was about Monica's height. Well-built and wore tight sport shirts. This showed that he liked to show off his muscular physic.

He did have that, that's for sure.

With his black hair and thick mustache, he resembled a younger version of Tom Selleck.

He dropped his rake and walked across the street. Smiling. He held out his hand. He introduced himself as Hank. "Heard you met my wife last night?"

Meet was not the word for it. "Yes. We did. Very nice." Though she was a little seductive.

"Good. She spoke highly of you two. She's excited we have new neighbors. House has been empty for a couple years. Nice to see some new faces around."

"I think it's going to be nice to be here."

"Oh, you're going to love it."

She couldn't help but notice the way his brown eyes roamed over her body. Like they were taking in every inch of her. For some reason it didn't bother her and she found it quite flattering. "I'm sure we will."

"I'm sure she probably mentioned our club?"

"She brought it up. Seems nice."

"Nice to get people together you know. With everybody working hard and with family and things it's nice to slow down, have a couple drinks with a few neighbors and get to know each other."

"That sounds nice." She was certain there was more to those two than meets the eye. Then thought maybe it was only her imagination.

Though the more she took notice of him in his spandex, it was obvious he wasn't shy about his well endowness. It was as if he wanted all the women to know how well hung, he was. Janet still couldn't refrain from taking a quick glance. She put her hand over her mouth to hide the smile on her face as she thought about how open he and his wife were.

"Good," he said. "I think you and your husband will have a good time. He fingered the gold necklace around his neck. "I'll talk to your husband about it."

He leaned in and gave her a peck on the cheek. She could smell the Axe Cologne as his chest softly brushed against her breast. His hand around her waist snugging softly but not too firm to be too intrusive but yet still too forward, enough to make her uncomfortable. Then at the same time a giddy feeling of warmth swept through her body.

Later Hank took Allen out for beers and discussed the whole arrangement. It wasn't what Allen had thought it was. In fact it he didn't know how they could call it a club at all. And he had an even harder time believing something like that existed. But it had his curiosity and what Hank had told him did make some sense.

Janet listened as Allen explained the club. It was simple. Every Saturday night, a letter arrives in your mailbox with the address and time of the partner you are to swap out with for the night.

Janet thought this sounded insane.

Really?

He said Hank had told him that ever since he and his wife started up this club, they have saved over a hundred marriages. Hank talked to him about how it added that extra spark to their sex life, increased their way of living and brought them closer together than they ever thought possible. Not to mention all the various positions and evening activities one brings to the table. Think about how much we all can benefit from each other's experiences.

"So, you would do this?" Janet asked.

"I think so. After listening to what he had to say. I believe I would. What can it really hurt? There are no strings attached. Just neighbors working together to improve on our sex lives and our relationships."

Janet did remember reading an article in a magazine written by a Dr. stating how it is very healthy to have an affair every once in a while. The Dr. Must've known what they were talking about because she had all these credentials in marriage counseling and had been in practice for twenty years.

"I don't, Allen. This sounds a little..." She wasn't sure what the word for it was.

"Insane? Nutso?"

"Yeah. I mean to actually sleep with another person. That would be having an affair," Something she never saw herself doing.

"I know. But that's the fun part of it all. Nobody cares. The neighbors don't mind. They're all for it."

I don't know Allen. You're going to have to give me some time to think about this one."

"I understand. But Hank said their meeting up again on Saturday." He grabbed a beer from the fridge. "Seriously, though. I think this is going to be a blast."

"What. You telling me you don't mind me sleeping with somebody else?"

He took a pull of his beer. "No. Not really. It's not like you're gonna be in love with the guy. Besides, maybe he'll be able to teach you a few things to pleasure me." He giggled like this was permission to have a fling. "It's not really an affair either. It's not like we're sneaking around to do it."

"This just sounds too creepy."

"You're seriously thinking about doing this?"

He took another pull of beer. Then another. "Yeah. I think it's going to be a blast. I've heard about this before, just not with an entire neighborhood. If we decide it's not for us we just won't do it anymore."

Still, Janet wasn't fully convinced about that club. She had to admit, she'd never saw Allen so excited about something in a long time. The way he smiled and walked around and acted all giddy.

After speaking with a few of the neighbors about this club and listening to what they had to say about it she agreed to go through with it. They did share in her concern about it being the first time but they assured her she would not regret it. Each of them had their own experiences to share.

One said her husband was more alive now than he ever had been in his life.

Another said her husband was far much happier.

Another said that her husband has learned some things that make her go Ohhhhhhh. All night long. And I had learned some things as well.

The benefits are endless.

For one, it added excitement to their week. Gave them something to look forward to.

Second. They were able to share different sexual positions, things most of them never thought of. Positions that would make your jaw drop.

Third. Everybody is in agreement. No harm. No foul. Just some fun sex. Nothing more. Nothing less.

Marci, one of the neighbors who'd been a club member for three years now said there was only one rule.

Once you receive your envelope you have to have sex. No matter what.

Actually, there's another part of that rule one. If you're a new member. You have to have sex. So watch for your envelope in the mail.

After all. That's really what this is all about.

Still, Janet couldn't help but feel uneasy about the whole thing. If it wasn't for Allen being so gung-ho about it she probably wouldn't go through with it. Mostly, she was shocked that he didn't mind the two of them having a one-night stand.

And that Monica?

What was up with her?

She saw the way her eyes roamed all over her husband as if she were studying his manhood as a scientist would study for a project.

Hank wasn't any better. One couldn't help but take notice of the way lustful eyes looked at her.

The more neighbors she spoke with, the more she discovered the entire neighborhood was involved in this club.

All seemed to have perfect marriages and couldn't say anything bad about what they were doing. While she was a little girl it was considered taboo to do such a thing and often resulted in immediate divorce.

When she brought her concerns up to Allen, he didn't become furious, instead he seemed to become more irritated in the fact that she didn't want to do it.

He didn't understand why.

It was obvious everybody in the neighborhood was happy.

He told her the same as he did earlier. Just give it a shot and if it turns out it's not for us then we'll stop.

She received phone calls later or some of the other ladies would stop by and ask her if they were going to participate in the club.

So anxious to get them involved.

So anxious it was creepy.

Allen told her it was just her imagination.

Something was wrong with this. Surely, there has to be some hidden consequences.

It was that following Saturday when Janet received a letter in the mail from the club.

"That was quick," Allen said.

Janet thought it was probably a little too quick.

Allen watched eagerly. "Open it. Let's see who you get."

"Open your first."

Allen cut the envelope open with his pocketknife and pulled out the letter. Janet knew who he'd gotten by the expression on his face.

"Let me guess. You got Monica?"

"How'd you know?"

"Wild guess."

Not to mention the fact that her eyeballs were crawling all over Allen's crotch the entire time she was here.

"Your turn," He says.

Janet opened hers, unfolded the paper and bit her lower lip. "Charles Ray."

"Who's that?"

"I don't know. Obviously, he's a neighbor."

She fantasized about Charles being six foot tall with long black hair. Something about long hair in men turned her on.

She was in for a chock when she walked up to the house and realized that Charles Ray was the old man that was watching them from the window of the house across the street.

The one with the rotten teeth.

Now, she was having her doubts. Allen gets the hot chick, and she gets the shriveled up old man.

What gives?

She'd settle for the hot chick over the old man any day.

Changing her mind she walked away but was stopped by a deep raspy voice.

"Please. Don't change your mind. You're gonna love it."

Janet thought, okay, she'd heard it all now. Talk about ego. "It's just I'm kinda tired. Maybe another day."

"No, you're not. I'm not what you expected, and you changed your mind."

"It is getting late."

"Please." He opened the door wider. "Come in."

This guy was really starting to creep Janet out but. There was no way their sex life was going to benefit.

I'll pretend I'm going to go along with it and escape. That's what I'll do she thought. Just entertain him a bit. After all the guy is at least eighty. How much can he really do at eighty?

He guided her to the second floor and brought her into the second room on the left. It was a beautiful room. Flowery wallpaper, old but still in good shape. The wood trim work was dark brown, and the room smelled of Carnations.

"Wait here. Make yourself comfortable. I'll get us a drink."

She smiled and nodded.

The dressers were made of real wood and not that fake particle board crap that most are made of today. The bed was high and the mattress so thick you needed a step stool to climb up into it.

Yet she couldn't help but think that there was something creepy about this old man.

Something strange.

Skeletons hidden in the closet.

She opened the closet expecting to find some skeletons but instead saw five or six photo albums.

She opened it.

Her eyes widen at the sight.

There were pictures of men on men. Women on women.

Another picture was him doing somebody from behind. She tried looking closer to see who the woman on her knees was but the image of too blurry.

Another picture was of him doing a woman who was decapitated. He was holding her head in his right hand. Holding it high in the air. As she looked closer, she could see the blood had been dripping at the time of the picture.

She gagged at the sight.

She didn't want to look anymore. But now she didn't have a choice.

She closed the book and picked up another,

The next filled with the same kind of gory pictures.

One of them was of him holding the head of a blonde haired girl with his penis in her mouth. Janet could see the girl's body lying on the bed in the background.

The next one was Monica and her husband Hank with a woman in between. Monica had a huge chunk of flesh in her mouth. The woman was tied to the bed and Hank stood above her holding a knife.

In at least every other picture was a woman she recognized from the neighborhood.

They're all in on it, she thought.

She thought of Allen and who he was with right now.

She opened the door to run out to see the old man standing there with a plate full of cookies and a bottle of wine.

"Sorry it took me so long, my little sweetie pie. Forgot where I had stashed the wine."

"it's okay" She covered her mouth. 'I think we're going to have to take a rain check. I'm not feeling well."

"Why. What's wrong?"

"Must've come down with a bug all of a sudden. I'm very sorry."

"I'm sorry to hear that," he said. His eyes glanced toward the wall, and he saw the closet door was open. "Ohh, I see. You must've found the pictures."

She charged past him, knocking him over. She heard the plate clashing on the floor and the wind bottle breaking.

She ran out into the street and charged right into Allen who was just on his way to Monica's house.

"They're all murderers!" She said. "The entire neighborhood. They're murders."

She explained to Hank what she saw and told Hank that they had to get out of there. There was no time to pack or nothing.

Hank was arguing with her, telling her this was all her imagination and that everything was going to be fine. She didn't have to make it with the old man if she didn't want to.

It was then Monica and Hank came out.

Then came the rest of the neighborhood. Walking down the street chanting. "Chop 'm up... Chop'm up.... M M.... Goood.

All carrying hatchets and machetes. Blood dripping from the blades.

"I get the blonde with the big penis," Monica said.

"I get the chick with the big boobs," Janet heard the old man say.

"They are going to be sooooo tasty," a neighbor said. "I just love new neighbors."

Allen and Janet screamed as a machete blade sliced across their throats in unison.

The next day a FOR SALE sign was placed in front of the house.

RONALD IS A BAD BOY

Ever since Ronald stabbed his five-year-old sister, Beth, it didn't take a brain surgeon to realize there was something wrong with Ronald.

His mother, Janet, came in as Ronald was stabbing and jabbing. Smiling. Laughing. Giggling in that creepy childlike voice he that creeped her out so much.

His sister screaming, crying, pleading for Ronald to stop because it hurts.

Ronald laughing and giggling, having the time of his life.

Fortunately, Janet walked in at the right time but not before Ronald managed to get at least twenty stabs in her legs.

"Ronald! What are you doing?" It was a stupid question but one that always came up first when confronted with these types of situations. It's one of those, am I seeing what I'm really seeing type of things. This was not normal behavior for a ten-year-old boy.

He looked at mother. "I'm staaaaaabing my sister."

He wasn't even afraid to tell her that he was stabbing his sister. It didn't appear to bother him or disrupt him in any way.

This is just sooooo sick.

She got Beth away from her stabbing brother and put Ronald in his room and then went about patching up Beth which she'd done for the fifth time now.

She felt so sorry for Beth.

Her husband, John said it was just kids being kids and didn't seem like it was a big deal that he liked to stab things.

She knew something was wrong from the second he turned one and liked to stab at his teddy bears and tear big holes in them and laugh and say things like, 'how you like that Teddy-Weddy? Mama is going to be pissed.'

She pulled her skirt up over her kneecap revealing several scars and puncture wounds. At least twenty of them.

Then it hit her. Was it possible he was stabbing her leg while she was sleeping? Even John was waking up with marks on his legs.

Several times she'd wake as she felt like something had bitten her leg. It would often leave a tiny pin hole with a little blood trickling down her thigh.

John shared a similar experience.

Some nights she would feel it and other nights he would.

Their first thought was that maybe it was bedbugs. He spent some time checking the beds and mattresses but never found anything. And their mattresses didn't have springs as he'd remembered when he was a kid.

Not once did it cross their minds that Johnny was stabbing them in their sleep.

Beth's dolls took a good stabbing as well. Many times, Beth would bring one of her dolls to her mother crying as they had fallen victim to Ronald's stabbing. He enjoyed slicing off the fingers and toes of her dolls and stab them in the middle of their stomachs.

She didn't know where he was getting the knives. How could such a young sweet boy that everybody loved be so much into stabbing things?

She didn't leave her knives out. Never did.

He always seemed to find something to stab with. It really wasn't that difficult to find something to do some stabbing when you really want to.

She found him doing it with pencils. Once he unfolded a paper clip. A thumb tack. Though those only left mostly punctures.

There had been times he took the pictures off the wall and took the nail out and used that to stab with.

After a serious discussion with her husband, they came upon the decision that they had to make the house as less stab proof as possible.

But how do you do that?

They were afraid to do a google search over such a thing. Too many people watching what you're searching for these days. The last thing they needed was for child protection services to come knocking at their door wanting to take Ronald away.

Couldn't talk to friends.

What are you going to say? How do you make your house stab free? Yeah, like that won't draw attention.

So, they set about with an attempt to make their house as stab free as possible.

Didn't make sense. Most new parents had to worry about making their house childproof for safety. There wasn't anything written in a child development handbook about what to do if your child is into stabbing.

Not that anybody is really going to ask such a crazy psychopathic question.

Janet called the school and told them; Ronald was very sick and wouldn't be in for a few days. This bought them some time and also kept the school system off their backs.

They locked Ronald in his room while they performed this crazy task. They removed all pencils and pens scattered throughout the house. They collected two shoe boxes full of things they collected from her husband's desk and in several dresser drawers.

The everything drawer had the most items. Everything from paper clips to pencils and pens to tacks of various types. Even screws and a handful of nails. Yeah, he could do some damage with those.

The two of them couldn't believe all the things they had around the house for Ronald to stab with.

It was insane.

They spent the entire day going through the house. Janet crying practically the entire time, upset and scared.

Just when they thought they were done and was about to relax, Janet saw the family picture on the wall.

Forgot something.

They commenced in removing all the pictures off the walls and took out all the nails.

Not only that, she had John take the pictures and put them up in the attic when she realized the frames could be taken apart where the pointed end of the corners could be used for stabbing, like a stake.

Janet thought, it just goes to show that you don't realize how many dangerous objects are around your house.

John felt after going through all this, he could do a little stabbing for himself.

They were tired. Exhausted. Janet wondered how long this so-called fetish of his would last or if they were ever going to be able to get him over it.

Or would this lead to other things?

Was their son truly a psychopath?

No. She wasn't going to allow it.

A fingernail file sat on the end table. She cursed as she grabbed it and tucked it away.

Is this ever going to end?

Seems like the house had a never-ending supply of things Ronald could stab with. The two of them never realized their house was so dangerous.

It wasn't just stabbing objects they had to tuck away either. There were plenty of things for Ronald to be a bad boy with.

He also liked to smash things. Smash his sister's doll heads.

His sister came to her mother crying, showing a doll with a flattened head that Ronald smashed with a rock.

A time came when Ronald had settled down and it had been a few days since his last episode and things were all quiet and fine until she got home one day from school and saw Ronald twirling Felix by his tail.

The poor cat screaming its head off as Ronald twirled it round and round. She didn't know how the cat managed to escape Ronald's wrath but he some how did and made of the door. They never saw or heard from Felix ever again.

Ronald always apologized and even though there was no way of ever bouncing back from his behavior he somehow managed to charm them over and get his parents to take him and his sister out for ice-cream.

Taking him out was the last thing they really wanted to do but John and Janet wanted to give Ronald a chance and they didn't want to disrupt him.

Beth was the one that wanted to give up and put Ronald in some kind of home but , John said there was no way and even though he is a wicked little boy he was still their son. He reminded her that Ronald was the son he always wanted.

John insisted they ride this out and said these things have a way of working their selves out in due time.

They weren't sure if Ronald heard them talking about him or not because all of a sudden, he was a good boy.

He started doing more chores around the house.

He kept his room clean.

He even washed his dishes when he was done and for Janet, that in itself was a big improvement for a child is age.

It was yes sir and no mam.

It was both cute and great but yet unsettling all at the same time.

Could it be, she thought, maybe this whole thing with Ronald was coming to an end? They certainly hoped so because they didn't know how much more they could take and even if they were capable of holding Ronald back any longer. They could only pray that he was going to be okay from here on out.

If not, Beth thought maybe they could take Ronald to the priest and get the demon taken out of him. Ronald was making the exorcist look like a sissy.

It was hard because they both had full time jobs. John kept various hours at the real estate company and had to go away a lot meetings. She was a substitute teacher at a school that Ronald was supposed to go to, so quite often she had to lock him in his room until she got home and this worked for a while. Sometimes she would get home and find Ronald sitting on the couch watching TV and was in awe at how he was able to get out.

It wasn't unusual for her to take several days off so she could stay home and watch Ronald. They didn't dare try getting a babysitter. Lord only knows what Ronald would do then.

She'd taken off so much she used up all her sick days and vacation days. It only made sense for John to keep going to work being that he was the one that brought home the most bacon.

Finally, the school quit calling her and the time she did check in with them in hopes of getting some hours they told her they found someone else.

Just like that. She was fired. Not really fired. Just told they no longer needs her services that way they don't have to pay any unemployment.

To make things a bit worse, John's office was told they all had to take a pay cut for a couple months until things got back under control. Even though this was normal in the trucking industry and often the problem was resolved fairly quickly it still came at a bad time.

Their car payments were late and so was everything else.

A couple months passed, and it appeared that Ronald was holding true to being a good boy.

Things at John's office started looking better and they got their original pay back with an extra bonus which helped catch them up on the car and house payment.

The school was suddenly in need of more substitutes and called Janet back hoping she was still available.

By now, Ronald was about twelve. John thought he was old enough and well-behaved enough to stay home by himself as long as he stayed inside and kept the doors locked.

So, they had a nice little sit down with little Ronald and discussed the do's and do nots of staying home by yourself. Ronald smiled and said that he could do this and for the first time in a long time, Janet and

John felt good about things and were happy that for once it looked like Ronald's whole stabbing thing was coming to a halt. This gave some relief but still they felt like they couldn't drop their guard. Janet thought about asking a neighbor, Martha, to keep an eye on him and since, Martha was unaware of Ronald's bad habit she would be the most likely candidate.

John, however, didn't think that was such a great idea and thought that would bring unwanted attention so he decided it was best that he take a couple days off and stay home with Ronald. Beth liked John's plan and felt instant relief.

Their problem was solved.

Janet went to work and for the first time in a long time felt relaxed and comfortable.

John was right. What was she thinking?

John always told her that it was just a mother being a mother.

She had the best day she'd had in a long time. Things went well at school. Her fellow teachers and the principle asked how Ronald was doing and she told them just fine.

Until that night she walked in the door and saw Ronald stabbing Beth with a pair of scissors.

There was no screaming.

Just Ronald giggling as he stabbed...stabbed...and stabbed.

Pluck pluck.... He stabbed her eyes.

In the throat.

Three times in the heart. She could hear Beth's ribs cracking.

STAB...STAB...STAB...

Beth's body jolted and jerked.

Janet's mouth widened with a frozen scream. One that rose up from her gut and blocked her airway.

It all happened so fast as little chunks of Beth flew off from the scissors.

John sat in the chair reading a paper. Dried blood on his fingers and she could see the bloody fingerprints on the paper.

"Hi, Mommy," Ronald said looking up. His mouth full of blood. "It's okay. Mommy. Daddy killed Beth so I could play with her longer.

Don't miss out!

Visit the website below and you can sign up to receive emails whenever Christopher Ridge publishes a new book. There's no charge and no obligation.

https://books2read.com/r/B-A-RYTC-IKSJC

BOOKS 2 READ

Connecting independent readers to independent writers.

Did you love *Shouldn't Play with Dead Things*? Then you should read *Creatures*[1] by Christopher Ridge!

[2]

A five story collection of horror and science fiction creature stories. Big bugs destroying towns. Insects in outer space and creatures out at sea. These creature stories are fast paced and quick short reads. Some are light-hearted and some are gory and you can always count on a lot of action and destruction.

Read more at creaturecritter.blogspot.com.

---

1. https://books2read.com/u/3k2dng

2. https://books2read.com/u/3k2dng

Also by Christopher Ridge

Hairy Scary Eight Legged Engineers
HOME INVASION
Bug Spray not Included
DateBite
Giant Steel Death Machines
The Ugly Truth About Shopping Carts
Dead End Job
Lobster Woman of Bubwater
Hatchet Hall
There's a Man on that Street
CUT'M UP TALES
Severance
The Fling
Macabrre Monthly
Strikeout
Splat
Slime
Because Google Said
Demented Tales
Captive
The Ghost Pirate
Clickety Clackers
Bumper to Bumper
The Hatch
Help Wanted

Creatures
Shouldn't Play with Dead Things

Watch for more at creaturecritter.blogspot.com.

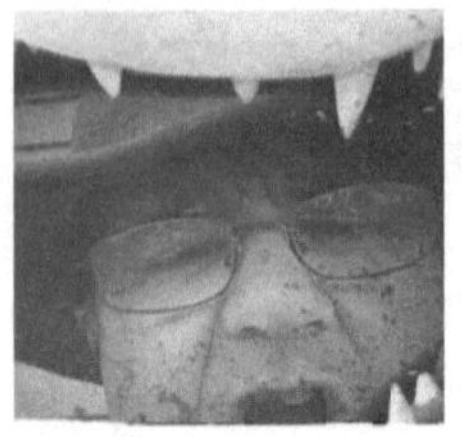

About the Author

Christopher Ridge is a creature feature horror and sci-fi writer. He enjoys B horror movies, aliens, monsters and mutant insects and such. To get an idea of what his stories and short novels are like think ATTACK OF THE KILLER TOMATOES, THEM, and IT CAME FROM OUTER SPACE. He lives in Indianapolis Indiana with his wife and two sons.

Read more at creaturecritter.blogspot.com.

About the Publisher